THE EXTRAORDINARY GARDENER

Sam Boughton

TATE PUBLISHING

Joe was a boy with a wild imagination.

It took him far away to a world less ordinary,

to a place very different from ...

the world outside.

In Joe's world, plants grew taller than skyscrapers,

and animals unlike any other roamed the streets and soared through the sky.

Every day, Joe longed
for his world
to come to life.

Then one night,
while he was reading
his favourite book,
an idea began
to grow.

It was full of beauty,
colour, scent and song,

and it all started with
something very small.

The next morning, Joe went in search of the one little thing that would bring his idea to life.

He looked in all the usual places,

and the not so usual.

Finally, he found
what he was
looking for.

Wasting no time, Joe collected all his tools together
and carefully planted the tiny seed.

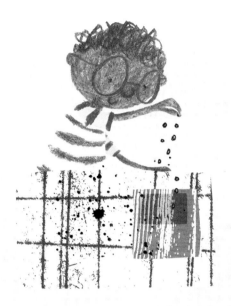

Then he fed it,

and watered it,

and quietly waited ...

and waited ... and waited some more.

But nothing happened. Nothing changed.

Eventually, Joe stopped waiting. He forgot all about his seed,
and he went back to what he knew best: imagining.

But something
was happening.

The seed had begun to grow.

It grew
and grew …

and GREW.

Then one ordinary day, while Joe was busy daydreaming, something colourful caught his eye.

He stepped outside and discovered that where he had
planted the tiny seed now stood the most beautiful tree.

Joe got to work at once.
He learned to preen and
prune, dig and sow.

Every day, he brought home
new seeds. He started to grow
all sorts of things.

Before long, the single tree
had become a tiny garden
that grew bigger …

and bigger …

and BIGGER!

One by one, Joe's neighbours
came to visit his beautiful garden.

When Joe saw his new friends so happy,
he had another idea.

Joe decided to share his garden
with people throughout the city.

And slowly,

over time,

with the help of that first tiny seed,

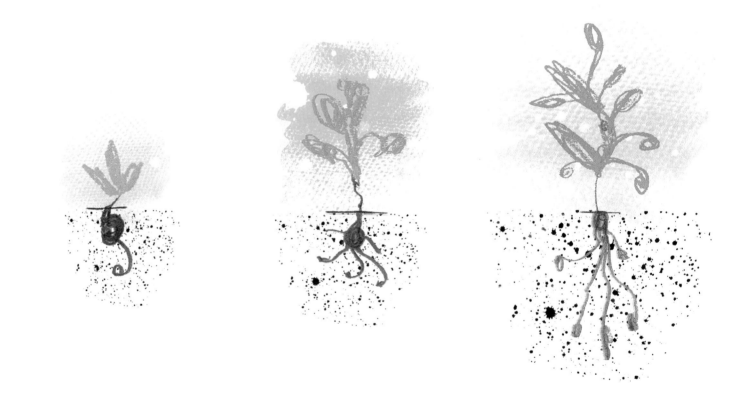

Joe's world grew from ordinary to . . .

EXTRAORDINARY!

For my loved ones, who make my ordinary
become extraordinary ~ S.B.

First published 2018 by order of the Tate Trustees
by Tate Publishing, a division of Tate Enterprises Ltd,
Millbank, London SW1P 4RG
www.tate.org.uk/publishing
Text and illustrations © Sam Boughton, 2018

A catalogue record for this book is available from the British Library.
ISBN 978 1 84976 566 4
Distributed in North America by Abrams Books for Young Readers,
an imprint of ABRAMS, New York.
Printed and bound in China by C&C Offset Printing Co., Ltd.
Colour reproduction by Evergreen Colour Management Ltd.

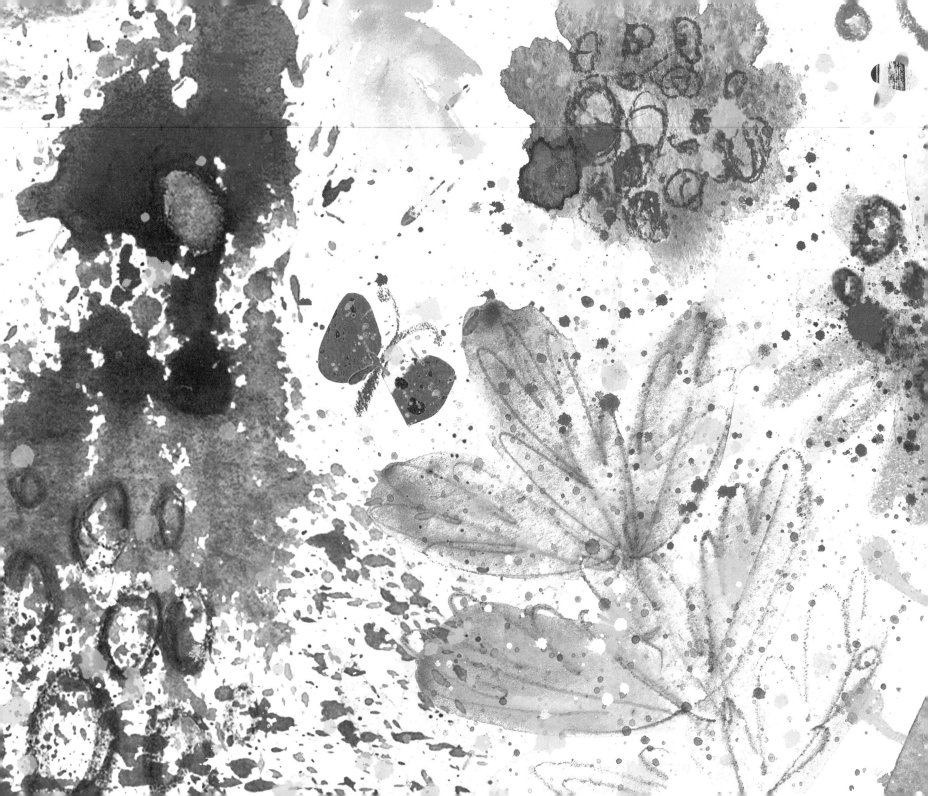